Ellie's Birthstone Ring

Beatrice Gormley

Ellie's Birthstone
* Ring *

ILLUSTRATED BY
KAREN RITZ

Dutton Children's Books
NEW YORK

Text copyright © 1992 by Beatrice Gormley
Illustrations copyright © 1992 by Karen Ritz
Library of Congress Cataloging-in-Publication Data
Gormley, Beatrice. Ellie's birthstone ring / by Beatrice Gormley;
illustrated by Karen Ritz.   p. cm.
Summary: As she makes plans for her seventh birthday party,
Ellie must decide whether or not to invite an older girl who
lives nearby. ISBN 0-525-44969-8 [1. Friendship—Fiction.
2. Birthdays—Fiction.]   I. Ritz, Karen, ill.   II. Title.
PZ7.G6696E1 1992 [Fic]—dc20 92-17259 CIP AC
Published in the United States
by Dutton Children's Books,
a division of Penguin Books USA Inc.
375 Hudson Street, New York, New York 10014
Designed by Adrian Leichter
Printed in U.S.A.
First Edition
1   3   5   7   9   10   8   6   4   2

to Karen,
the first to listen to this story

CONTENTS

Ellie's Birthstone Ring

★ O N E ★

A Birthday Coming Up

I'm *never* going to get to the variety store," Ellie called to her mother from the front steps. "Justin's still asleep."

Ellie felt so antsy she could hardly stand still. In two weeks, it would be her birthday. Today at the variety store, she was going to pick out invitations and plates and napkins for her party. Ellie jumped from the top of the front steps to the bottom. She wished she could jump over two weeks that quickly.

Mrs. Lang was on her hands and knees by the mailbox, planting daffodil bulbs. "Sure you'll get to the store." She squinted at her daughter against the bright October sunlight. "I just want to finish these bulbs. By that time, the baby will be awake. Or Dad will be through cleaning the gutters."

Of course, Ellie knew that as soon as her baby brother woke up, her mother would put him in the stroller. Then the three of them would walk to the store. That's what they did most Saturday afternoons. But . . .

In two weeks, I'll be seven! thought Ellie. She did a little dance on the flagstone walk: *one*-two, *three*-four, *five*-six, *seven!* Six quarters, her allowance, jingled in her jeans pocket.

On Saturday mornings, Ellie cleaned up her room and helped watch the baby. Then she went to the supermarket with her father and recycled the bottles. After lunch, Ellie and her mother or father, sometimes with Justin, walked down the hill and along Old Post Road to the variety store. Her parents bought a magazine, but Ellie spent her allowance on candy or stickers or maybe a comic book.

But today's trip wasn't so much for spending Ellie's allowance. Today Ellie would skip past the candy and stickers and comic books at the front of the store, straight back to the party goods. Goods for her own party, the Saturday after next.

Stooping, Ellie handed her mother an onion-like daffodil bulb from the bag. Ellie liked to help her mother garden. She usually pretended that they were pioneers growing their crops. But today, her birthday filled her mind. "Mom, what was it like on my zero birthday?"

Her mother took the bulb and set it into the damp earth. "What was it like when you were born? Well, it was pretty exciting. . . ."

Ellie had heard the story of how she was born many times. Grandma had to take Mom to the hospital because Dad was at work in the city. Dad had rushed into the birthing room just in time to see Ellie come out.

Ellie glanced over her shoulder at the roof of

the house. Her father was cleaning the gutters with the buzzing leaf blower. "Dad said — " she prompted. She knew what Dad had said, but she liked to hear her mother tell it.

"Dad said, 'She's just born and already I have to run to keep up with her,' " said Mrs. Lang.

"So that's who came to my zero birthday party," Ellie went on.

"Right. Dad and Grandma and I." Ellie's mother smiled at her. "Grandma looked at you and said — "

"She said," Ellie chimed in, " 'Our baby is a little jewel!' "

"You know the story by heart." Ellie's mother laughed and dug another hole with her trowel.

"This year," said Ellie, "I want to have a sleep-over party, like Bonnie did." She handed her mother another bulb.

"Okay," said Mrs. Lang. "But then you can't invite the whole class. Three friends would be about right."

Ellie pictured Mrs. Butterfield's classroom

with all the kids in their seats. This was like a homework problem: Draw a circle around each animal with spots and a tail. Only Ellie's problem was: Pick out the right girls for your birthday sleep-over party.

To Ellie's surprise, it was easy. In her mind, three girls already had circles drawn around them. They were the three, besides Ellie, who liked to play pretend games at recess.

"Nina Pagnano," said Ellie. "*If* her mother will let her come. And Caroline Fong, and — "

Ellie was about to say "Bonnie Carraway" when she noticed Ruth strolling down the hill toward them. Ruth lived two houses up the street. She was in the fourth grade, but sometimes she came over to play with Ellie.

Smiling her big smile, Ruth waved at Ellie. Ruth must not have a school friend over today, the way she usually did on Saturdays, thought Ellie. Or maybe Ruth was on her way to a friend's house, just passing by.

Ruth stopped near the mailbox. "Hi, Mrs.

Lang." Ruth's big front teeth flashed, and dimples came out in her cheeks. "Hi, Ellie. See my watch?" She held out her wrist.

Ruth's watch had a clear wristband, a green rim around the face, and a flock of glittering stars under the hands. "The stars go around once a minute," she explained. "It's just like Jennifer's. She was so mad when Daddy bought me one, too. So — what're you doing?"

Ellie wasn't sure why Ruth was asking. Was she just curious, or did she want to do something with Ellie? Ellie never knew when Ruth would feel like playing with her.

"In a minute, we're going to the store," said Ellie. "When Justin wakes up."

"Great," said Ruth. "I'll come with you."

Ellie grinned. The times that Ruth did decide to play with Ellie, it was a lot of fun. Then Ellie had an idea. "Mom — I could walk to the store with just Ruth. You said I could walk with a friend when I turned seven. And I *am* turning seven."

Her mother hesitated. "But you're still six."

Before Ellie could argue, Ruth spoke up. "Yeah, my mother said the same thing when I was six. She would *never* let me walk to the variety store without her. In fact, she was worried sick. She said 'Sweetie, what if a kidnapper drove up in a van and grabbed you off the street? I'd never forgive myself.' "

Ellie's mother raised one eyebrow. "Well, all *I* ask is, be careful of the traffic on Old Post Road. I'm talking about that part where there isn't any sidewalk. Walk single file, all right?"

"Yes!" exclaimed Ellie. She put up her hand toward Ruth for a high five.

Skipping downhill beside Ruth, Ellie took deep breaths of the clear air. Last Saturday, Ellie had stood by her mailbox and watched Ruth strut down the hill with a school friend. They'd snapped their fingers and leaned from side to side in time to their rap song:

> Well, we're walking to the *store*
> And we'll buy our *gum* . . .

Ruth had smiled and waved at Ellie, as always. But then she and her friend had turned the corner onto Old Post Road and disappeared.

Now it was Ellie turning the corner with Ruth.

✷ T W O ✷

The Birthstone Ring

On the first stretch of the busy road, Ellie followed Ruth. Ellie pretended she was a pioneer girl following her Native American guide to the trading post. She tried to walk without making any noise, but the dry leaves crackled under her feet.

"You're in Mrs. Butterfield's class, right?" asked Ruth over her shoulder. "She always loved my stories for News of the Week."

"I know; she likes everyone's stories," said

Ellie. "She's pretty nice." Ellie didn't usually feel like getting up in front of the class for News of the Week, though.

"When I was in the second grade," Ruth went on, "Mrs. Butterfield said to my mother, 'Mrs. Jasper, Ruth brings a *ray of sunshine* into this classroom.' " Ruth giggled.

Ellie laughed, too, but in a puzzled way. It didn't sound like something that sensible Mrs. Butterfield would say.

"Follow the leader!" called Ruth. She ran up onto a lawn and turned a cartwheel. Her legs whirled through the air like spokes. Her long braid swung out from her head. She landed on her feet with her arms out, smiling to an invisible audience.

Ellie knew her cartwheel wouldn't be that good. But she plunged toward the grass before she could get nervous. Her legs went up in the air pretty straight. But then she felt her quarters sliding out of her jeans pocket, and she pulled her legs down too soon. She tipped backward and barely managed to land on her feet.

"Yay, Ellie!" Ruth clapped, just as if Ellie had turned her best cartwheel. She pretended to hold up a scorecard. "Nine point five!"

Ellie laughed and shook her head. Ruth was nice. A lot of kids would have tried to make her feel bad about such a clumsy cartwheel. Ellie slid her hand into her pocket to check on her quarters and touched a half roll of Life Savers. They were left over from last Saturday.

Life Savers were Ellie's favorite candy. She liked to pull the little string to open the roll. She liked to pry the jewel-colored rings of candy out of the wrapper one by one. She liked the tart-sweet taste of red cherry Life Savers and orange Life Savers and green lime Life Savers. But her favorite were the light yellow pineapple Life Savers.

The girls crossed a side street, and the sidewalk began. "My turn to lead," said Ellie.

"Oh, let's forget that." Ruth turned her big, dimpled smile on Ellie. "We're almost there."

As they stopped for the red light at the next corner, she pointed down the street to the dark red awning with the word VARIETY.

A few teenage boys were roller-blading back and forth in front of the store. Ellie recognized one of them — Ruth's older brother, Greg.

"I'm probably going to get licorice whips," said Ruth, "so Greg can grab a piece. Then he won't tease me for more. What're you going to get?"

"Probably stickers," said Ellie. "I need some for dress-up games, for badges and medals. And I still have some Life Savers."

The girls crossed the last street. "And guess what else?" asked Ellie. "I'm going to pick out invitations and things for my birthday party. It's going to be two weeks from today, at six o'clock."

"Really?" Ruth's face lit up. "Who are you going to invite?"

Ellie stared at Ruth. Could it be that Ruth wanted to be invited? Ellie had never been invited to one of Ruth's parties. In fact, she'd only been to Ruth's house a few times. And those were times when Ruth's older sister Heather had looked after both of them, last summer. Ruth had never actually invited Ellie over to play.

But maybe things were different, now that Ellie was turning seven and could walk to the variety store with just Ruth. Maybe the next time Ruth had a party, Ellie would be invited. She wouldn't have to look up the street at the balloons tied to Ruth's mailbox and feel left out.

"For one thing," Ellie said slowly, "I'm going to invite — you!"

Sure enough, Ruth looked pleased. Then she had to dodge her brother. He was reaching out to poke her as he zoomed past on his roller blades. Ducking into the doorway of the variety store, Ruth grinned at Ellie. "Me? That's nice! I'll help you pick out the invitations and things."

The variety store was long and narrow. After

the bright sunlight, it seemed dim inside, like a cave. Ellie loved the sweet, exciting smell, partly from the candy in front of the cash register and partly from the comic books on the wire rack.

"Hello, Ruth," said Mrs. Bayer. For the longest time, Ellie had thought the name of the lady in the variety store was Mrs. Bear. Not that she *looked* at all like a bear.

"Hello, Ellie," Mrs. Bayer went on. "What's new? Where's your mom, your dad, and your baby brother?"

"I came by myself," said Ellie. "I mean, with Ruth."

Mrs. Bayer nodded, her eyes widening. "That's what's new! You're getting to be big stuff."

Ellie blushed proudly, giving the comic-book rack a spin. "So what's new with you?" she asked.

Mrs. Bayer pointed to a display at the end of the counter. "Those rings just came in."

Ellie walked slowly over to the display, a

black velvet rack. This was like discovering treasure in a cave. Four rows of gold rings on the black velvet. The jewel in each ring sparkled a different color.

They were all the colors in a roll of Life Savers, thought Ellie, and some besides. Red, orange, green, yellow, blue and blue-green, pink and purple.

"Ellie," said Ruth. "Look at these new headbands."

Ellie glanced over her shoulder. Ruth was trying on a sequined headband in front of a little mirror. "You should look at these new rings." She turned to Mrs. Bayer. "How much are they?"

Mrs. Bayer peered over the top of the velvet rack to read a price tag. "You like the birthstone rings, do you? They're two ninety-eight apiece. With tax, that would be three dollars and fifteen cents."

Birthstone. That sounded as if each ring was meant for a certain person, from the moment

that person was born. Ellie stared at the rings with the colored jewels and felt the six quarters in her pocket. Six quarters were only a dollar fifty.

"Oh, birthstone rings!" Ruth appeared at Ellie's shoulder. "Pretty. My birthday's in May — emerald." She pointed to a ring in the second row, the one with the green jewel. "That would match my watch." She held up her wrist to show the bright green rim around the watch.

"My birthday's in November," said Ellie.

"That would be topaz." Mrs. Bayer pointed to the ring in the middle of the bottom row. Its light yellow jewel was the color of a sucked-thin pineapple Life Saver.

Ellie read what it said on the rack, under that ring. "November people are brave and self . . . self . . ."

"Self-reliant," finished Mrs. Bayer.

"Come on, Ellie," said Ruth. "Don't you want to look at the birthday stuff?"

Self-reliant, thought Ellie. She knew what

that meant — like the pioneers. They did things for themselves, like building their own cabins and making their own soap and drying apples for the winter.

Ellie followed Ruth down the aisle. Maybe she could ask for the ring for her birthday. But that was two weeks away, and she wanted the ring right now.

Saving Up

*M*aybe the Little Mermaid," said Ellie, pointing. She stopped in front of the back wall of the store. The party plates and napkins and invitations and loot bags were lined up on the shelves in matching sets. Ellie and Nina and Caroline and Bonnie had played the Little Mermaid at recess, wiggling all over the playground. The trouble with that pretend game was, everyone wanted to be the Little Mermaid.

"You like those?" asked Ruth doubtfully.

"Sets like the Little Mermaid or the Teenage Mutant Ninja Turtles seem more for little kids. Hey, you know what everybody's doing now? Cows!" She pointed to a package of invitations with black-and-white cows.

"*Cows?*" Ellie could hardly believe that, but Ruth must know. Actually, none of the sets seemed just right. Maybe her parents would take her to another store, or maybe her mother would help her make invitations.

"I don't *have* to decide today," Ellie finally said. She turned away from the party supplies. "I'm going to look at the stickers."

On the way to the stickers, Ruth stopped to try on headbands again. "Look at this one, Ellie. I bet it would look cute on you, too." She fitted a yellow headband with rows of stiff ruffles over Ellie's front hair. "And they're only three forty-nine."

"But all I have is a dollar fifty," said Ellie.

"I don't mean buy it yourself. I'm going to get my mother to buy one for me." Ruth patted the sequined headband on her own hair. Then she put on a serious face, as if she were Mrs. Jasper, her mother. "Now, Ruth, I can't buy you everything you ask for. . . . If you want the headband, why don't you save up for it? . . . Oh, all right."

Ellie had to laugh. She remembered one of her times at Ruth's house. Mrs. Jasper had been trying to rush out the door, leaving Ruth and Ellie with Ruth's sister Heather. Ruth had been begging to stay up and watch a movie on TV.

"Now, Ruth," Mrs. Jasper had said. "Sweetie, you know those scary movies give you nightmares. . . . And besides, it's on much too late. . . . Oh, all right."

Ruth sure knew how to get around her mother. But begging didn't work with *Ellie's* mother.

Stepping past Ruth, Ellie looked up at the rolls of stickers. A couple of weeks ago, she'd bought gold stars. She'd stuck one of them on her brother Justin's head. She'd pretended that he was a fairy baby, marked with a magic star. Ellie liked being the oldest in her family.

Ruth was the youngest in hers. Ellie had seen Heather and Jennifer, Ruth's other big sister, laugh at things Ruth said. They exchanged glances over her head and snickered. Ellie would hate that.

Ellie's gaze shifted from the stickers to the black velvet rack at the end of the counter. The ring in the middle of the bottom row flashed its light yellow jewel at her. *Topaz. Birthstone.*

Ellie sighed. No, her mother wasn't like Mrs. Jasper, who would buy things if Ruth begged her. Or like Mr. Jasper, who had bought Ruth her watch. Ellie had heard her own mother say to her father, "If you ask me, the Jaspers should give Ruth fewer things and more attention."

Then something Ruth had said popped into Ellie's mind. The words seemed to be meant for her now. *Why don't you save up for it?*

Ellie could save up for the topaz birthstone ring! She could save the six quarters in her pocket now and put them together with the six quarters she would get next Saturday. Then she'd have twelve quarters. That was three dollars. And the pile of pennies in the bottom of her piggy bank would pay for the tax.

"What kind of stickers are you going to get?" Ruth interrupted Ellie's thoughts. "The cows are cute, aren't they?"

"I'm not going to get stickers," said Ellie.

"Oh, candy, then?" Ruth picked up a package of licorice whips from the candy rack.

Ellie shook her head. "I'm going to save my money."

Mrs. Bayer leaned over the counter, smiling at them. "That's right, Ellie. You're smart. Save your money. Save your teeth."

Ruth looked annoyed, but she walked out of the store without saying anything.

The minute the girls were on the sidewalk, they heard a shout from down the block. "Feeding time!" It was Ruth's brother, Greg.

Ruth sighed. "I *have* to give him something or he won't leave me alone." She paused on the sidewalk to open her licorice whips. Breaking one in half, she held it up like a dolphin trainer holding up a fish. "By the way, Ellie, I thought *you* were going to get something to share."

Ellie stared at Greg and stepped out of the way. He grabbed the piece of licorice as he zoomed past on his roller blades. "What? Oh, I do have something to share." Ellie dug the half roll of Life Savers from her pocket. "I told you, I already had Life Savers. The reason I'm saving my money is — "

" — because you're such a smart little girl!" said Ruth in a gruff voice like Mrs. Bayer's. She laughed and nudged Ellie. "Just kidding." Ruth strode along the sidewalk, waving a fresh licorice whip like a bandleader's baton.

Ellie marched fast, lifting her knees to keep up. She unpeeled the red cherry ring from the top of the Life Saver roll and offered it to Ruth.

"Thanks," said Ruth. "Watch this." She

tossed the ring into the air and caught it in her mouth.

The orange Life Saver was next in the roll. Ellie tried to do the same trick with it. But the candy ring bounced off her chin and rolled into the gutter.

"Too bad," said Ruth cheerfully. "Here's a licorice whip. Hey, pretend you're a dentist looking at my teeth."

"Okay. Open wide, Ruth." Ellie held her licorice whip like a dentist's pick and poked the end of it into Ruth's mouth. She started talking like a dentist. "Now, Ruth, you know that candy is *very bad* for your teeth — yow! What are you doing?"

Ruth bit the "dentist's pick" off. Ellie laughed so hard that she doubled over.

The two girls walked single file along the last stretch of Old Post Road. Ellie bounced through the dead leaves. Ruth could come to her house and play for the rest of the afternoon. They could practice tricks on the gym set. Ruth liked Ellie's gym set, with the look-out tower at one end and the rungs across the top. Or maybe Ruth would ask Ellie to play at Ruth's house for a change.

No — Ellie knew just what she wanted to do with Ruth. She'd been thinking of building a log cabin in her backyard. Ellie actually had logs — or rather, the big stack of firewood under the porch. All she needed was someone to help her lift the heavy chunks of wood and stack them into walls.

They turned the corner onto Copper Beech Lane. Ruth glanced over at Ellie, and Ellie noticed that Ruth had finished her licorice whips. Quickly Ellie peeled the paper off the last two Life Savers.

The Life Saver on top was pineapple, her favorite. She knew she could pop it into her own mouth and give Ruth the cherry Life Saver. But instead, she placed the light yellow candy ring on Ruth's palm. "Here you go."

"Thanks," said Ruth. She flipped the candy

into her mouth and crunched it up. Ellie sucked her cherry Life Saver slowly, to make it last.

As the girls reached Ellie's mailbox, Ellie began, "Hey, you know what we could do?"

But just then a green car rolled down the street toward them. Ruth's sister Heather was driving.

Ruth jumped up and down and waved. "Heather! Heather!" To Ellie she said, "I bet Heather's going to the mall."

The car stopped beside the girls. Ruth's sister leaned across the seat to roll down the window. She shouted over the music from the car radio. "What? I can't stop — I have to go to the mall."

"Good!" said Ruth. "Bye, Ellie." Before Ellie could answer, Ruth pulled open the car door. She jumped into the front seat beside her sister. "Don't worry, Heather. I won't bother you."

Heather rolled her eyes at her little sister.

Then she sighed. "Oh, all right." She waved toward Ellie with a baby-sitter's smile. "Hi, Ellie-kins! Bye!"

Ellie stood beside her mailbox and watched the green car turn the corner and disappear. She pressed the cherry Life Saver, thin as glass now, against the roof of her mouth. Too bad she hadn't gotten a chance to explain the pioneer game. Ruth might have stayed. Or she might have asked Ellie to come with her to the mall.

✴ F O U R ✴

News of the Week

On Monday morning, Ellie waited for Nina to walk through the classroom door. The moment her friend appeared, Ellie pounced on her. "Guess what? I can have a sleep-over party!"

"Yes!" exclaimed Nina, slapping Ellie's palms.

"We'll have dinner and the cake and watch a movie," Ellie went on. "But I can only invite three kids."

The two girls slid into their seats next to each other. Ellie took her birthday party list from the inside pocket of her Trapper Keeper. She had already printed MY BIRTHDAY PARTY at the top of the paper and stuck a gold star on each side of the heading.

As Nina watched, Ellie printed: *1. Nina Pagnano*. Then she drew a stick figure with bright pink stretch pants and matching hair bow, like Nina's.

"That's me, all right," said Nina with a grin.

But Ellie gave her friend a sudden fierce look. "Only you have to promise, *promise* you won't let your mother ruin everything."

Nina stopped smiling and drew back. "How can I help it if my mother makes me visit relatives?"

"You've got to because it's not fair." Ellie was still mad when she thought about what had happened a few weeks ago. "Like when your mother said you could sleep over, and we had it all planned. And then she called up and said you couldn't come! Just because you had to go to your aunt and uncle's Columbus Day party."

Nina sighed. "I know, I know. I'll talk to her. But don't blame me. *She's* the mother and *I'm* the kid, right? Anyway, who else?" She pointed to Ellie's list.

Ellie started to write Caroline's name. But then she remembered she'd already invited Ruth.

"Who's Ruth Jasper?" asked Nina, watching Ellie print the name.

"A girl on my street." Ellie spoke in a matter-of-fact voice, as if she'd always expected Ruth to come to her birthday party. She moved to the next line and wrote: *3. Caroline Fong.* "I haven't told Caroline about my party yet," she added.

The girls both looked across the room at Caroline. She was stooping to fuss with Bonnie's hair, taking out her barrettes and fastening them in again. At the same time, Bonnie was waving her arms and talking.

They're like a big sister and a little sister, thought Ellie. She could imagine why Caroline would like *having* a little sister. But why would Bonnie like being *treated* like a little sister? Especially since she was small to begin with.

Ellie started to add Bonnie's name to her list. Then she stopped with her pen in the air. "Uh-oh." There were already three names on her birthday party list. But Bonnie fit in with Ellie and Nina and Caroline. "Maybe my mom will let four kids come," said Ellie finally. She printed Bonnie Carraway's name on her list under Caroline's name.

The bell rang, and Mrs. Butterfield collected the homework. Ellie tried to imagine her teacher calling someone a ray of sunshine, the way Ruth said she had.

"This is Monday, class," said the teacher. "And you know what that means."

"News of the Week!" several kids called out.

Ellie had forgotten about Mondays and News of the Week. But now, without even trying, she thought of some news she wanted to tell. Her hand flashed up.

"Mrs. Butterfield!" exclaimed Caroline. "Let Bonnie go first — she has a killer story."

"Then Bonnie should put up her own killer hand," said the teacher with a smile. She nodded to Ellie, and Ellie stepped to the front of the room. "Yesterday I tried drying apples, like the pioneers," Ellie began. "I sliced up an apple and spread the slices on top of the radiator behind my bed."

"The pioneers didn't have radiators," Jeremy called out.

"Ellie is speaking, and we're all listening politely," said the teacher. "This fits in with the story we're reading about pioneers, doesn't it? Only they dried their apples in the sun. I'm interested to know how Ellie's apples turned out."

Ellie grinned. "Well, they never got dried. First they turned brown and mushy. Then somebody left my door open, and my baby

Monday, Oc
1. News of th
2. Arithmeti
3. Recess
4. Reading
5. Computer
6. Lunch

brother, Justin, crawled behind the bed. And then my mother and I heard his slobbery eating noises."

Some of the kids in the class made slobbery noises. A lot of them were laughing.

"The apples were so gross," said Ellie. "Justin bit every single slice. And I had to clean up the mess."

"I think Ellie learned something about pioneer life." Mrs. Butterfield smiled at Ellie. "I'm sure the pioneers had the same kind of problems with drying fruit. Maybe children like you would have to watch the fruit, to keep birds and other animals from eating it."

Ellie went back to her seat, feeling proud. The teacher looked around. "Who else has news to tell?"

"Oh!" said Nina, waving her hand. But the teacher called on Bonnie next. Bonnie giggled behind her fingers as she dragged her feet to the front of the room.

"My news story is about — " Bonnie looked

out the window. She jumped in place, as if she were trying to jiggle her words out.

"About what happened at dinner last night," called Caroline.

"Let Bonnie tell," said Mrs. Butterfield.

"Okay, I can tell," said Bonnie. "See, my little sister won't eat vegetables. And my mom and dad try a lot of different things to get her to eat them. So last night she said she'd eat her peas if she could roll them down a tube, the kind of tube in paper towels."

"Roll them down a tube!" Ellie looked at Nina, and they burst out laughing.

"So she started rolling the peas one by one." Bonnie tipped her head back to show them. "And she really did eat three in a row."

All the kids in the room were laughing. Nina waved her hand in the air again.

Mrs. Butterfield laughed, too. "That's a funny story, Bonnie. Now I think it's time for arithmetic."

"Wait, the best part's coming," said Caroline.

Bonnie went on. "My sister started laughing about rolling the peas down the tube. And she breathed one in and choked. My dad had to turn her upside down and smack her on the back. And the pea flew out of her mouth and landed right in the dog's water dish!"

The class screamed with laughter. It took the teacher a few minutes to get everyone quieted down again.

Then several other kids wiggled their hands in the air. But Mrs. Butterfield held up her hand for silence. "Those were — er — killer stories, but we need to get on with our work. Please take out *Three — Two — One — Blast Off!*" She began to write an arithmetic problem on the board.

$$6 \text{ quarters}$$
$$+ \underline{6 \text{ quarters}}$$

"How many quarters?" asked Mrs. Butterfield.

Ellie remembered how her six quarters' allowance had fallen with six clinks onto the pennies in her piggy bank. And next Saturday, after chores, her father would hand Ellie six more quarters. This was amazing, just as if the teacher knew that Ellie was saving up.

"I'm saving up for a birthstone ring," whispered Ellie to Nina.

"If you know the answer," said Mrs. Butterfield, "put up your hand. If you don't, please — Yes, Ellie. How many quarters?"

"Twelve," said Ellie.

"Yes!" Mrs. Butterfield always looked so happy when someone said the right answer. She wrote *12 quarters* on the board. "Now, who knows what twelve quarters equal?"

"Three dollars!" exclaimed Ellie, forgetting to raise her hand. The teacher called on Caroline, and Caroline gave the same answer.

Ellie whispered to Nina, "Want to come to the variety store on Saturday? That's when I'm going to buy my birthstone ring."

✻ F I V E ✻

Just a Little Kid?

*E*llie set her lunch tray down next to Nina, across from Bonnie and Caroline. "Let's play Pioneers today at recess — want to?"

Nina looked up and nodded. Her mouth was full of tuna-salad sandwich. Bonnie frowned as if she wasn't sure.

But Caroline seemed to be thinking about something else entirely. "They shouldn't give us tuna-salad sandwiches on Monday," remarked Caroline. She tucked Bonnie's napkin in her lap for her. "Tuna is fish, and they're supposed to have seafood on Fridays, not Mondays."

"But tuna isn't seafood," said Bonnie. "Seafood means things like fried shrimp or fish sticks."

"Tuna is fish, though," said Ellie. "So it must be seafood."

"That reminds me," said Nina, "I didn't get a turn at News of the Week."

"*Seafood* reminds you of News of the Week?" asked Caroline. "What do you mean?"

"Listen, I'll tell you." Nina grinned and cleared her throat. "You know, my big brother, Ricky, has terrible table manners. Like last night, he was chewing with his mouth open."

"I've seen him do that," said Ellie. "Ee-yuck."

"And my dad said" — Nina broke into giggles — "my dad said, 'I'm tired of having seafood dinners every night.' And my mom said, 'What do you mean, seafood? This is meatloaf.' And my dad said" — more giggles — "my dad said, 'Because I can *see* the *food* in Ricky's mouth!' "

"*See* food!" Ellie laughed so hard that she rocked back and forth on the bench. Bonnie laughed so hard she choked. Caroline patted her on the back.

"So tuna could be *s-e-e* food, anyway," said Ellie. The girls began to eat their tuna sandwiches, chewing carefully with their mouths closed.

After lunch, Ellie followed Nina and Caroline and Bonnie onto the windy playground. "We're playing Pioneers, right?" asked Ellie. "We can gather nuts and berries because the winter is coming."

"Yeah!" said Nina. "But I wish we could bring dress-up clothes to school. My mother might let me have her old prairie skirt."

"I'll play," said Bonnie eagerly, "if I can be Dorothy."

Ellie and Nina stared at Bonnie, then at each

other. "Dorothy?" asked Ellie. "What are you talking about?"

"She means Dorothy in *The Wizard of Oz*," Caroline explained. "Because Dorothy was a pioneer. I've got dibs on being Glinda, the Good Witch."

"Dorothy was not a pioneer!" exclaimed Nina. "This is all wrong."

Nina liked things to be right, but Ellie cared more about getting them to play her game. "No, wait — this will work," she said. "We'll play Pioneers *and* Fairies."

"Pioneers and fairies do not belong together," said Nina.

"But pioneers and fairies are alike in a lot of ways," argued Ellie. She was sure that was true because she felt the same way about them. But she couldn't think just how they were alike. "Oh, come on and play!" Ellie started to lead Nina and Caroline and Bonnie across the playground. "See all the acorns under those trees?" she called, pointing. "Let's gather them."

Then Ellie noticed some older girls lined

up for jump rope. She recognized Ruth by the light brown braid hanging down her back. Ruth was leaning toward the girl on her left, a shorter girl with a long blonde braid.

Dimples dented Ruth's cheeks as she begged, "Let me go before you — please-please? You're so good, you'll jump forever, and I'll *never* get a turn."

Ellie was going to hurry on toward the oak trees. But just then, Ruth glanced over her shoulder. As she caught sight of Ellie, a big smile spread across her face. "Hi, Ellie!" Ruth waved.

"Hi, Ruth!" Ellie felt the grin on her own face. Ruth's smile was like a traffic light flashing WALK. Without thinking, Ellie started walking toward the jump rope line.

The blonde girl next to Ruth turned around. If Ruth's face said WALK, her friend's face said GET LOST. "I wish there was a rule against first graders bothering us," said the girl to Ruth. "Who's that?"

With a flick of her long braid, Ruth turned

back toward the jump rope. Ellie stopped where she was. A gust of wind blew grit in her face.

Ellie hoped Ruth would say, "Don't talk about my friend Ellie like that." Or even, "Ellie's in the *second* grade. We walk to the variety store together."

Instead, Ruth said in a low voice, "Oh, just a little kid on my street."

Ellie felt her face grow warm. She glanced around to see if her friends had heard. But they were gone, as if the wind had blown them away.

Across the playground, Nina was jumping into the sand around the swings. Caroline and Bonnie were already swinging, side by side. "The flying monkeys got us!" they shouted to Nina.

Ellie shouldn't have wasted time with Ruth. She'd only gotten her feelings hurt. And meanwhile, Caroline and Bonnie and Nina had slipped into *The Wizard of Oz*. Now Ellie would never get them to gather acorns.

When Ellie came in from the playground after recess, she took the birthday party list from her Trapper Keeper. She took a sharp pencil from her pencil box. Then she crossed Ruth's name off her birthday list.

Pioneers
and Fairies

"Winter is coming," Ellie told Justin. "The wolves might prowl right up to our cabin."

It was the end of the week, a cool and cloudy Friday after school. Ellie was watching her baby brother while their mother cleaned leaves out of the flower beds.

The good thing about Justin, thought Ellie, was that you could play any pretend game you wanted with him. Right now, she was thinking of building the walls of her log cabin around his playpen.

Justin threw his teething ring out of the playpen and looked at Ellie. "Ah ha-ha!"

Ellie picked up the ring, brushed it off on her sweater, and dropped it back into the playpen. "Next time, a wolf will grab it. Then you'll never get it back."

Justin shoved the teething ring into his mouth. Ellie stared thoughtfully at the firewood under the porch. The pieces of wood were too heavy for her to lift off the ground by herself. Too bad Nina wasn't coming over until tomorrow. But maybe Ellie could pick up one end of a log and drag it over to the playpen.

I'm self-reliant, thought Ellie. Tomorrow I'll get my allowance and put it together with last week's allowance. I'll go to the variety store with Nina. Then, *finally,* I'll buy my birthstone ring.

Ellie held out her hand, imagining the topaz ring sparkling on her finger. Just the thought of it made her feel stronger.

The telephone rang inside the house. Across the yard, Mrs. Lang let her rake fall and hurried toward the steps. "I'll get it, Ellie."

Ellie wondered if it could be Nina on the phone for her. She hoped not. She didn't want Nina to call and say that her mother wouldn't let her come over tomorrow.

Justin threw his teething ring out of the playpen again. Ellie tossed it back in, ran over to the woodpile, and tugged at a loose log.

Panting and grunting, she managed to drag it across the grass and roll it up to the bottom of the playpen. Justin watched her with round eyes and open mouth. He forgot to throw his teething ring.

As Ellie turned back toward the woodpile, Ruth strolled around the corner of the house. She was smiling her big smile. "Hi, Ellie. Hi, there, Justin!"

Ellie stared. Ruth? Here in Ellie's yard? This didn't fit with the Ruth that she'd seen last Monday on the playground at school, whispering to that mean girl with the blonde braid.

Ruth leaned over the playpen to make a face at Justin. Then she noticed the log. She tapped it with one foot. "What's that for?"

Ellie leaned forward eagerly. This was just what she'd wanted last Saturday — the chance to work on the log cabin with Ruth. "I'm building — " But she stopped. "I have to watch Justin," she said.

"Oh, we can watch Justin and play at the same time," said Ruth cheerfully. "Want to practice tricks on the gym set? We'll take turns." She started for the ladder.

Ellie's heart beat faster. She wanted to play with Ruth. At the same time, she wanted Ruth to understand how she felt. "You don't really want to play with me," she muttered at the ground.

Ruth gave her a puzzled smile. "What do you mean? I came *over* to play with you."

"I thought I was too *little* for you." Ellie was still looking at the ground. She was afraid she was saying too much, and now Ruth would leave. She cast a sideways glance at Ruth. "At least, I thought I heard you say I was little. At recess."

Ruth stared at Ellie with wide eyes. "At recess? We didn't even go out for recess today." Then she shrugged and smiled. "Maybe you just *thought* I said something about you. A lot of words sound alike. Maybe you thought you heard me say 'Ellie,' but I said 'jelly.'" Ruth gazed across Ellie's yard at the yellow chrysanthemums by the back fence. The dimples appeared in her cheeks. "And maybe you thought I said 'little,' but really I said 'piddle.'"

Ellie had to laugh. Ruth laughed, too. Maybe Ellie had heard wrong, after all. Ruth wouldn't be here now if she didn't want to play with Ellie.

"I'm playing Pioneers," said Ellie. "Want to help me build the log cabin?" She pointed to the stick of firewood. In case Ruth wasn't interested in pioneers, she added, "We could play Pioneers *and* Fairies, if you want."

Laughing again, Ruth shrugged. "Sure! I'll be Tinker Bell." She danced across the lawn on her toes, twirling. She waved a hand toward the woodpile. "Look, I'm sprinkling fairy dust. Now the logs will be easy to carry."

The logs *were* easy to carry, with Ruth and Ellie lifting together. Ellie told the story they were acting out:

"The Pioneer Girl and Tinker Bell worked hard to finish building their cabin before sundown." She motioned to Ruth to turn the second log before they placed it on top of the first. "They skillfully fitted the logs together to make the walls of the cabin snug and tight."

As the log cabin grew around him, Justin began to whimper. "Don't cry, little pioneer baby," said Ruth, in a high Tinker Bell voice. "You can't have everything you cry for." To Ellie she said, "Let's stop. My hands are sore."

"All right." Ellie's hands were sore, too, but she hated to stop. She lifted Justin out of the playpen and jounced him until he laughed. At least, she thought, the square of stacked logs did look like a real half-built log cabin.

"I'll fly to the top of the stockade and be the lookout," said Ruth. She leaped up the ladder of the gym set and posed at the top with her arms out. It was getting dark, and Ruth turned into a shadow against the pink clouds.

"You know," Ruth went on, "Christine says I'm second-best in our class at gymnastics, next to her."

"Who's Christine?" asked Ellie. She wondered if that was the girl with the blonde braid.

"Christine Fuller. She can do no-handed cartwheels and back walkovers and flips. She might be in the Olympics when she's older. She has a private coach."

"Ru-uth!" Someone was calling from up the street.

"Is that your sister?" asked Ellie.

"Bummer! The enemy found us." Ruth giggled. "I mean, Heather's calling me for dinner." She dropped to the ground. "Want to walk to the variety store tomorrow?"

"Yes!" said Ellie. Then she added, "But I don't know. My friend Nina's coming over."

"That's all right," said Ruth. "We can all go together. Bye!"

Ellie wasn't sure Nina would like that, but maybe it would be all right if Ruth just went to the variety store and back with them. "Okay. . . . Bye."

As Ruth left through the neighbors' backyard, Ellie's mother came out of the house. She peered from the top of the porch steps. "It got dark so fast! Ellie, can you bring Justin up? We'll leave his playpen there for now."

Ellie lugged her baby brother up the steps and handed him to her mother. The Pioneer Girl's eyes were used to the dusk. But her mother hadn't even noticed the cabin.

Inside the house, Ellie went to her room and took out her Trapper Keeper folder. She wrote Ruth's name on the birthday party list again.

* S E V E N *

Ruth's Friend

*E*llie woke up on Saturday to see pale light coming in her high bedroom windows. She wondered if it would be another cloudy day. But Ellie didn't feel cloudy or pale. She felt bright and self-reliant.

It seems like my birthday, she thought. Only it's my *birthstone* day. She seemed to see the ring turning in the air just out of reach. Its yellow jewel flashed like sunlight.

After breakfast, Ellie called Nina. "Did you ask your mother if you could come over this afternoon? My father said we could pick you up on the way back from the Shop-Rite. And you can sleep over, too."

"I can't come over this afternoon," said Nina. "Don't get mad! My cousins from Chicago are visiting my grandma, and we have to go see them."

"I can't stand it," groaned Ellie. "You *always* have to do something with your relatives. It's worse than homework."

"I know," said Nina. "But maybe I can sleep over, anyway. Hold on."

Nina left the phone, but she was back in a minute. "My mother says I can come after dinner."

"What about my birthday party?" Ellie was suddenly worried. "Can you come to that?"

There was a pause. Then Nina said, "I told my mom when your party was. She said we'd see. Probably I can come."

"Nina!" exclaimed Ellie. "If you really want to come, make her promise."

After Ellie hung up, she started on her first Saturday chore, cleaning up her room. She was surprised, every Saturday, to find how many things had gotten scattered around. She picked a pair of socks from the arm of her wall lamp and put them in the laundry bag. She pried a squished Fig Newton from the rug and put it in the wastebasket. She noticed a library book making a square lump under the bedspread and stopped to look at the book.

The cover of the library book showed a man peering into a cave full of treasure. Dad and Ellie were reading this book, one fairy tale every night.

The book reminded Ellie of the ways that she thought fairy stories and pioneer stories were alike. She made a list in her mind:

- *Both happen in the woods (sometimes).*
- *Both need old-fashioned costumes.*

- *You have to be brave in both of them.*
- *You cook over fires in both of them.*

Ellie had tried to explain these things to Nina the last time she and Nina and Caroline and Bonnie had played at recess. But Nina had wasted a lot of time arguing. She didn't want to think pioneers and fairies could be in the same game.

"Ellie?" Her father stepped through the doorway. "Are you finished with your room? We're supposed to take down a log cabin. Some fly-by-night developer put it up in the backyard."

"My log cabin?" exclaimed Ellie. "Ruth and I went to a lot of trouble building it."

Her father looked at her in surprise. "I guess it must have been a lot of work. The trouble is, there are three reasons why we can't leave your cabin there." He ticked off a list on his fingers:

"One: We need Justin's playpen, which is stuck inside your log cabin. Two: The firewood will rot if we leave it out in the weather. And

it's starting to sprinkle right now. Three: The grass will turn brown and die if we leave the wood on top of it."

"Okay, okay! I guess we have to put the logs back," said Ellie. "And then we're going to the Shop-Rite, and I'll recycle the bottles. And you'll give me my allowance, right?"

That afternoon it was still cloudy, but the sprinkles had stopped. Ellie bounced up the street to Ruth's house, jingling twelve quarters in one pocket and fifteen pennies in another. This was like playing a game called the Pioneer Girl and Her Birthstone Ring — except it was really happening.

The only thing was, Ellie wished Nina were coming along. Then Ellie would have one friend on each side to watch her slide the birthstone ring onto her finger. Oh, well, Nina would see it tonight.

At the back of Ruth's house, Ellie climbed the steps to the deck. She peered through the sliding door into the kitchen. Suddenly she felt young and small.

Ruth's brother, Greg, was scratching his stomach under his sweat shirt as he drank cider from a quart jug. Ruth's sisters, Heather and Jennifer, were sitting at the counter. Heather was putting nail polish on Jennifer's fingernails.

"Hi, Ellie-kins." Heather waved the nail polish brush.

Did that mean come in? Ellie pushed the door open and stepped inside.

Jennifer twisted around from the counter. She managed to do it without moving the hand Heather was working on. "Ruth's having a friend over today, Ellie."

"I know — that's me," said Ellie. "Ruth's going to walk to the variety store with me."

Jennifer raised her eyebrows as if she knew better. Heather dipped her brush into the nail polish without saying anything.

Ellie waited. Should she just go to Ruth's room?

Before she could decide, Ruth appeared in the doorway to the kitchen. She was wearing a leotard. She looked surprised to see Ellie, but she smiled and waved.

Ellie grinned and waved back. Then she noticed the girl behind Ruth. She drew her breath in sharply. The other girl was wearing a leotard, too. And her long blonde braid hung over one shoulder.

Buying the Ring

The blonde girl stared at Ellie as if Ellie had made a bad smell.

"Hi, Ellie." Ruth walked across the kitchen, smiling a puzzled smile. "Christine's here, so — "

"But you said — " Ellie wished Ruth's big sisters and brother weren't right there, watching and listening. "I thought you said we'd walk to the variety store today."

Jennifer gave a little laugh. "Ellie thought Ruth would actually *remember* something. How quaint."

"Ree-tard Ruth," remarked Greg. He took another swig of cider.

"Oh, Ruth remembers what she wants to remember," said Heather. "Give me your other hand, Jen."

Ruth gazed at Ellie, acting as if her sisters and brother weren't there. "*I* said we should walk to the variety store?"

Ellie knew she would probably have to leave Ruth alone with her school friend. Probably she would just have to go home and get one of her parents to take her to the store. But it wasn't fair. *Ruth* was the one who'd asked Ellie to walk to the variety store.

Ruth turned to Christine with her big smile. She gave a little shrug of her shoulders. "Want to walk to the variety store, Christine? They have gorgeous new headbands there! And we could get Halloween masks. Heather will lend us the money until Mom gets back. Right, Heather?"

"Don't," said Jennifer to Heather. "That kid is getting so spoiled."

"I know," said Heather calmly, "but I can't help it. Sure, Ruth. Whatever your little heart desires."

Ellie thought if *she* had big sisters, and they talked about her like that, she'd start screaming at them. But Ruth said cheerfully, "Thanks, Heather." She went on to Christine, "So let's get dressed. We'll go to the store, and Ellie can come along. We'll finish the gymnastics meet afterward."

"All right — I guess." Christine was still giving Ellie that bad-smell look. "Just to the store and back."

A few minutes later, Ruth and Christine had jeans and sweat shirts on over their leotards. The three girls walked down the hill. Ruth, in the middle, glanced from Ellie to Christine as she talked.

"You know why I'll never get really good at

70

gymnastics?" asked Ruth. "My mother. I mean, she won't let me compete. She's afraid I'd get a sports injury. She said, 'If anything happened to you, sweetie, I'd have a nervous breakdown.' "

Ellie skipped to keep up with Ruth's and Christine's longer legs. "A nervous breakdown?" Ellie imagined Mrs. Jasper stopping in the middle of the street with a clanking noise. Ellie's father's car had done that once.

Ruth opened her mouth to explain, but Christine spoke first. "Where's your house, Ellie?"

"Right there," said Ellie, pointing. She was surprised that Christine was interested in where she lived.

"Well, why don't you go on inside?" Christine laughed. "It's time to watch 'Muppet Babies.' "

Ruth laughed, too, only in a nice way, as if Christine were just kidding. But Ellie wanted to give Christine a good kick in the shins, right where it really hurt.

More than ever, Ellie wished Nina could

have come over this afternoon. If Ruth had her school friend and Ellie had hers, they could walk two and two. Maybe then Christine wouldn't pick on her.

Never mind. They were turning the corner onto Old Post Road. Now they were walking single file, with Christine first and Ellie last. At least I'm not walking with Mean Christine, thought Ellie.

Once again, the Pioneer Girl followed her Native American guide down the trail to the trading post. Her hard-won coins weighted down the pockets of her calico dress. At the trading post, a rare birthstone ring lay in a treasure chest. The Pioneer Girl was brave and self-reliant, and the precious ring would soon be hers.

The girls reached the beginning of the sidewalk, and Ellie wanted to walk next to Ruth. But Christine took up all the room on purpose. Ellie had to fall back.

The awning of the variety store came in

sight. Suddenly a worrisome thought struck Ellie. What if someone else had already bought the birthstone ring for November? "Let's hurry," she said.

Over her shoulder, Ruth smiled at Ellie. But she was listening to Christine.

Putting a hand in one pocket so the quarters wouldn't bounce out, Ellie darted in front of the other girls.

"What's the matter with her?" said Christine. "Ants in her pants?"

But Ellie dashed on ahead. She crossed the last street by herself, yanked open the door, and practically leaped to the end of the counter.

"Whoa!" said Mrs. Bayer. "Where's the fire? Not in my store, I hope."

Ellie stood in front of the black velvet rack, panting. There it was. Her birthstone ring, its topaz jewel flashing at her.

Behind Ellie, Ruth and Christine came into the store, laughing. Ellie turned to show Ruth what she was going to buy. But the two girls strolled down the aisle without looking at her.

"Still thinking about those rings, huh?" Mrs. Bayer asked.

Ellie smiled a secret smile. "I'm not just thinking about them. I saved up. And now I'm going to buy the November birthstone ring." She took the twelve quarters and fifteen pennies from her pocket and lined them up on the counter.

"Well!" Mrs. Bayer opened her eyes wide. "Aren't you the hot ticket. Three dollars and fifteen cents, right to the penny." She turned the rack around and unfastened the November ring from the black velvet. Then she handed it to Ellie.

As Mrs. Bayer rang up the sale on the cash register, Ellie slipped the ring onto her finger. The fourth finger of her right hand, where her mother wore rings that weren't her wedding rings.

Ellie had really bought her own birthstone ring! She had planned to buy it. She had saved up without any help. And now she was wearing the November ring on her finger. She gave a sigh of satisfaction.

"Do you know how to adjust the size?" asked Mrs. Bayer. "That looks a little loose." She showed Ellie how to slide the thin part of the ring back and forth, to make it larger or smaller. Ellie tightened the ring so it was just snug.

"Enjoy!" said Mrs. Bayer.

Ellie turned her hand this way and that to make the yellow jewel sparkle. Yes, this ring had been waiting for her ever since she was born. Ellie had to grow up to be self-reliant and earn the money to buy it, but the ring was always meant to be hers.

Wait till Ruth saw this! Ellie glanced around the store. Ruth was at the far end of the aisle, trying on Halloween masks and making Christine laugh.

Now the older girls were strolling toward the front of the store. Ellie decided not to tell them what she'd bought. She would just let them notice the beautiful ring on her hand.

Ruth and Christine stopped to look at the

headbands. "You can't wear a headband like that when you do gymnastics," Christine told Ruth. "It would hurt when you did a forward roll."

Ruth shrugged and stepped to the candy rack in front of the counter. "Hey, let's get bubble gum and see who can blow the biggest bubble. I bet *you* blow the biggest bubble, Christine. Want to get bubble gum, Ellie?"

Ellie shook her head, but Ruth didn't notice. Oh, well. When they were outside in the daylight, Ruth would notice the birthstone ring, for sure.

Three Guesses

*E*llie skipped along the sidewalk behind Ruth and Christine. She held out her right hand to admire her ring. Even if Ruth didn't notice it by herself, sooner or later Ruth would wonder what Ellie had bought. Then Ellie would make her guess. Finally, Ellie would show Ruth the birthstone ring.

Ellie imagined how Ruth's eyes would pop. She would probably want her mother to buy her a birthstone ring. And probably her mother would. But that wasn't the same as saving up and buying it yourself.

Ellie would let Ruth try on the ring. She'd show her how to slide the thin piece back to make it fit. She wasn't sure she would let Christine try on the ring. Maybe for just a minute.

They were walking single file on the last stretch of Old Post Road. "Well, I guess I just blew the first-prize bubble," Ruth said to Christine. She turned her head and smiled at Ellie. There was a film of pink gum over her nose and cheeks.

"I'm tired of bubble gum," said Christine, rolling her gum off her face. She dropped it into a storm drain.

The girls turned the corner onto Copper Beech Lane. Ellie felt she'd better speak up now, or Ruth might not notice her ring.

"Ruth," said Ellie loudly. She stepped up beside her. "You get three guesses — what did I buy at the variety store?"

Ruth peeled off the gum mustache she had made and gave Ellie a surprised look. "I don't know. Life Savers?"

"Not candy." Ellie tried not to grin. She caught her breath with excitement. "Guess again. I'll give you a hint: It's something you know I wanted."

"Stickers."

"No. It cost more than that — three dollars and fifteen cents, with tax. Remember? I saved up."

Christine leaned over from the other side of Ruth. "Training pants." She laughed.

"Don't, Christine," said Ruth.

Ellie stared at Christine. Christine was really not very nice. Why was Ruth friends with her?

"Don't mind her," Ruth went on to Ellie. "She's down on little kids — her stepmother has three of them! Anyway, I don't know. What *did* you buy?"

Ellie smiled. "If you look at me, you'll find out." She held out her right hand, just a little.

Ruth's gaze fell on the ring. "Oh, that! I

didn't see you buy it." She laughed a little. "It's nice."

"It's my birthstone ring." Ellie stretched her hand out farther, turning it from side to side. "The jewel is topaz, for November, my birthday month. It means I'm self-reliant."

Christine leaned across Ruth to stare at the ring. "Topaz! Oh, *right*." She laughed and rolled her eyes. "You saved up to buy that junky little ring?"

"Shh!" Ruth nudged Christine. "You'll hurt her feelings. It's a nice ring, Ellie. It's just that it's not a real jewel."

The cloudy sky seemed suddenly lower and darker. Ellie pulled away from the two older girls. She put her hand behind her back. But she'd already seen the jewel turn dull.

"I don't want to make you feel bad," Ruth went on, "but a real birthstone ring would cost much more than three dollars and fifteen cents. That's just a ring for little kids."

Ellie couldn't speak. She felt as if she'd been punched in the stomach.

"Little kids who play pretend games," added Christine. "Aren't you the one who plays Pioneers and Fairies?" She laughed a loud, mean laugh. "You can pretend all you want, but that's not a real jewel." She glanced up at the darkened sky. Rain spots began popping out on the pavement. "Hey, Ruth, it's starting to rain."

"Uh-oh!" said Ruth. "We'll get soaked. We'd better run for it. Bye, Ellie!" She gave Ellie a smile and a wave. Then she and Christine dashed up the hill.

Ellie stood at the edge of the road by herself, watching Ruth and Christine disappear behind Ruth's hedge. Her face burned. She had thought she could buy a real birthstone ring for three dollars and fifteen cents. She had wasted two allowances. She wasn't self-reliant. She was just a stupid little kid who thought pretend games were real.

Raindrops spattered on Ellie's slicker. She put her right hand, the hand with the ring, into her slicker pocket. With her left hand, she pulled the hood over her head.

It was only half a block to her driveway. But by the time she got there, the legs of her jeans were soaked. They stuck to her knees at every step.

Ellie ducked under the open door of the garage, then stopped. There was the trash can in the corner. She ran to the back of the garage and tugged the lid off. Then she twisted the ring from her finger. A junky little ring, not a real birthstone ring. Ellie dropped it into the trash.

The Lost Ring

That evening, after dinner, Ellie stood on her bed and watched for Nina to arrive. She leaned her elbows on the sill of the high bedroom window and rested her chin on her hands.

The stuffed baked potatoes from dinner made a lump in Ellie's stomach. She'd had to shovel them down. Her mother thought she might be sick because she wasn't eating much. If Mom had decided Ellie was sick, she wouldn't have let Nina come over. Then it would have been a completely awful day.

There was a sore place inside Ellie, as if she really had been punched in the stomach. At dinner, she'd thought of telling her mother and father what Christine and Ruth had said about her ring. She knew her parents would try to make her feel better.

But then they would know that she'd saved two allowances to buy a junky little-kid's ring. She didn't want to let anyone know that.

Ellie saw a car slow down and turn into her driveway. She jumped down from her bed and hurried to meet Nina at the front door.

"Whew!" said Nina. She stepped inside with her overnight bag. "I thought I'd never get here. That mother of mine . . ."

Ellie smiled and shook her head. "Yeah, that mother of yours!" She could feel the day changing from awful to better, now that Nina was here. "Come on, let's go in my room."

Nina followed Ellie down the hall. "Did you

go to the variety store?" she asked. "Did you get that birthstone ring?"

Ellie flinched. Why had she told Nina she was going to get the ring? "Yes, but — I — I lost it," she muttered without turning around.

"Oh, no!" Nina pulled on her arm. "That's terrible! Let's look for it."

"It wasn't that great," said Ellie. She stepped into her room and changed the subject. "Did you ask your mother about my party?"

Nina nodded, beaming. "I made her *promise* I can come. And no changing her mind."

Ellie clapped her hands. "Yay! I'll check you off." She got out the birthday party list and put a big red check beside Nina's name.

Then Ellie looked at the bottom of the list, where she had written Ruth in again yesterday. Picking up the black crayon, she scribbled over Ruth's name. She scribbled until the letters were blanked out by a black cloud.

Nina was sitting on Ellie's bed, pushing herself up with her hands and bouncing. "At your party, after we watch the movie, want to play Pioneers?"

Ellie winced. She wasn't sure she wanted to play Pioneers anymore at all. "I don't know."

But Nina went on. "It would be great because you know what we could do? We could all bring our dress-up clothes. That would be so much better than playing at recess. Don't you hate it when the bell rings to go back in, just when the game gets good?"

"Yeah, I know," said Ellie. She thought of her list of the ways pioneer stories and fairy tales were alike. But she didn't feel like bringing that argument up again with Nina. "Anyway, want to make cookies? We got some Slice 'n' Bake chocolate-chip dough."

Ellie and Nina baked the cookies and took a plateful to Ellie's parents. Then they ate another plateful themselves while they watched *The Wizard of Oz.* "I can sort of see why Bonnie thought Dorothy was a pioneer," said Ellie as the movie ended.

"I guess," said Nina doubtfully. "But Bonnie

has some weird ideas. And Caroline always explains them for her, like a big sister."

Ellie looked at her friend in surprise. "I know — that's exactly what I was thinking."

As Ellie pushed the rewind button, her father appeared with the fairy tale book in his hand. "It's story time, am I right?" Then he pretended to have a second thought. "But wait — you girls just watched a movie. That was instead of hearing a story."

"It — was — not!" shouted the girls together. They pushed him toward the sofa.

Laughing, Ellie and her father settled into their comfortable dents in the sofa. Nina curled up on the other side of Mr. Lang.

"You have to come over more often, Nina," he told her. "It takes a lot of sitting to make your own dent."

"Maybe I could get fat." Nina giggled. "That would help."

Ellie's father nodded as Ellie opened the book of fairy tales. "Yes, that would help. All right — our story for tonight is 'Tattercoats.' "

"Tattercoats" was about a girl who was dressed in rags. But the prince thought she was beautiful anyway, and he fell in love with her. He introduced the ragged girl to his father and said he was going to marry her. And then her rags turned into shining, jeweled robes and a golden crown.

As Ellie listened, the birthstone ring seemed to appear before her eyes. All evening she had been trying not to think about the ring. But now she imagined it lying in the trash can in the garage. She felt bad for the ring, as if she had been mean to a person.

On the other side of Ellie's father, Nina wiggled deeper into the sofa cushions. "That story was awfully short," she said. "Maybe you could read another one, to make up."

Mr. Lang laughed. "All right. Ellie, do you want another story?"

"Yes," said Ellie, "but wait a minute." She slid off the sofa. "I have to get something. I'll be right back."

Before her father or Nina could ask any questions, Ellie hurried through the kitchen and down the basement stairs. She ran through the playroom and opened the door to the garage.

The garage was cold. The bare bulb overhead gave only a dim light. With a lump in her throat, Ellie walked around the car to the trash can in the far corner. She pried the lid off. The can was full of bags of trash. The smell of coffee grounds and rotten apples floated up. She didn't see her ring.

What if she couldn't find it? The lump in Ellie's throat rose into a sob. She lifted out one bag, and there, on top of the next one, was her ring.

Ellie bit her lip. In the gray light of the garage, the ring looked little and dull. No yellow rays flashed from the jewel.

But she couldn't leave her ring there again. Ellie picked it up and pushed it onto her finger.

As she climbed the basement stairs, the door at the top opened. "Ellie," called her father, "what are you doing?"

"I just had to get something," said Ellie. She stepped into the kitchen, blinking in the bright light. Nina was there waiting for her, too. Even Ellie's mother appeared, with Justin wrapped in a bath towel.

Nina gasped. "Your birthstone ring!" She seized Ellie's right hand. "You found it. It's beautiful!"

Ellie looked at her ring. She gasped, too. In the bright light of the kitchen, the yellow jewel flashed. Ellie held up her hand and wiggled her ring finger to make the jewel sparkle even more.

"Ah ha-ha!" said Justin. He leaned out of Mrs. Lang's arms to grab at the ring.

"Justin likes your ring," said Mr. Lang. "I don't blame him."

"It's a birthstone ring," said Ellie. "I bought it at the variety store, and then I lost it." She looked around at her mother and father and Justin and Nina, all admiring her ring. "But then I found it again."

☀ E L E V E N ☀

Happy Birthday, Ellie!

The Pioneer Girl with the Birthstone Ring watched from high above the trail. It was past sundown. Soon the other pioneers and fairies would arrive for her birthday party.

The Pioneer Girl's keen eyes could make out a bunch of yellow and green and red and orange balloons. They bobbed from the mailbox beside the trail.

I am seven years old, thought Ellie. She stood on her bed, steadying herself with one hand on the windowsill. Her birthstone ring sparkled on her finger. Any minute now, a car would drive up, and Nina or Caroline or Bonnie would arrive.

Then the doorbell rang, although there was no car in the driveway. Ellie leaped off her bed and raced through the hall, shouting, "I'll get it!"

She pulled the front door open. Sharp, cold air whooshed in.

"Happy birthday, Ellie." Ruth smiled a big, dimpled smile. She held out a present.

Ellie stood as still as if the chill air had frozen her. She couldn't speak. Why was Ruth here? Ellie knew she'd handed a special homemade pioneer birthday invitation to Nina, to Caroline, and to Bonnie. But Ellie sure hadn't handed an invitation to Ruth.

"But I crossed — " Ellie stopped. She *had* crossed Ruth off her birthday party list, but Ruth didn't know that. All Ruth knew was from two Saturdays ago. That was the first day they'd walked to the store together. That day, Ellie had invited Ruth to her birthday party.

Ellie stepped aside to let Ruth come in. But she didn't know what to think. Why did Ruth even want to come to her party?

"You look nice," said Ruth as Ellie closed the door. "That yellow top is new, right?" Ruth glanced at Ellie's right hand. "And it matches your ring! That's pretty."

For the second time, Ellie was too surprised to speak. Ruth thought Ellie's birthstone ring was *pretty*? The same Ruth who had said "That's just a ring for little kids" last week?

"Wait till you see what's in here!" Ruth held up a square package wrapped in paper with cows on it. "I got it at the mall. It goes on your wrist, and it has a guess-what-color jewel for guess-which month."

That could only mean one thing: Ruth had brought Ellie a *birthstone bracelet*. Ellie didn't understand at all. "But you said my birthstone ring was a junky little ring," she blurted out.

Ruth stared at Ellie. She let her mouth drop open. "I said what? No." Ruth's voice turned soft. "*I* wouldn't say that about your ring. Maybe it didn't cost very much, but it's a pretty ring."

Ellie was still mixed up, but she was getting surer of one thing, at least. Ruth wanted to be *some* kind of friends with her. "Well, but I know Christine said — " Ellie began.

"Oh, *Christine.*" Ruth laughed a little, spreading one hand as if she couldn't help what Christine did. "I know, sometimes Christine isn't too nice. You know what she said to *me* yesterday?" Ruth's eyes flashed. "She said I wasn't really that good at gymnastics! She even said I had bad form in my front walkover. And she said I had no hope of ever going to the Olympics."

Ellie struggled with herself. She didn't want to get in an argument with Ruth. But there was something important to say. "But when Christine was trying to make me feel bad, *you* just . . ."

Even though Ellie couldn't quite finish, Ruth looked uncomfortable. Ellie realized that she'd never seen that expression on Ruth's face before.

"*I* didn't want to make you feel bad," Ruth said finally. "I'm sorry, okay? Don't you want your present?" She held out the little square package again.

At that moment, Ellie heard hands and knees slapping the floor behind her. Her baby brother was in the kitchen doorway.

"Come back here, you little rascal." Ellie's mother scooped up Justin. "Why, it's Ruth. Hello. . . ."

Mrs. Lang looked almost as surprised as Ellie felt. What if her mother blurted out, "But Ruth — you weren't invited to Ellie's birthday party."

Ruth glanced from Ellie's mother to Ellie. Ellie thought how different and sort of sad Ruth looked right now, without her dimples showing.

Ellie took the present from Ruth. "Mom, I

made a mistake," she said. "I forgot to tell you — I invited Ruth, too, when we walked to the store two weeks ago."

"Oh — well, that's fine," said Mrs. Lang. "Come in, Ruth. Do you want to put your overnight bag in Ellie's room?"

Of course, Ruth didn't have an overnight bag. Ellie hadn't told her the party was a sleepover.

"Oh, I couldn't possibly stay overnight," said Ruth quickly. "My mother says I've been staying up too late. She's *so* worried I might get pneumonia, like I did last winter. She had to fly back from her business trip early. So she said, 'All right, sweetie, you can go to Ellie's party if you really want to, but don't stay too late. You have to take care of yourself because you know you have a tendency toward pneumonia.' "

"I guess you shouldn't stay overnight, then," Mrs. Lang agreed. As Ruth leaned toward Justin with a big smile, Ellie's mother gave Ellie a questioning look over Ruth's head.

Then the doorbell rang again. Ellie opened the front door with another whoosh of cold air. Nina was on the front step, hopping up and down. Behind her was Caroline, with one arm around Bonnie's shoulders. They hurried up the steps from the driveway.

Ellie noticed a denim ruffle — the prairie skirt — sticking out of Nina's tote bag. And Bonnie was wearing her hair in two braids with curly ends, like Dorothy in *The Wizard of Oz*. They would play Pioneers and Fairies after the movie, after Ruth had gone home. It would work out fine.

"Happy birthday, Ellie!" shouted Nina, and Caroline and Bonnie chimed in.

Ellie grinned so hard that it almost hurt. The Pioneer Girl's birthstone ring flashed as she waved her friends into the house.